Emerson and Princess Peep

By Valerie Tripp
Illustrated by Thu Thai

★ American Girl®

Published by American Girl Publishing

19 20 21 22 23 24 25 QP 12 11 10 9 8 7 6 5 4 3

Editorial Development: Jennifer Hirsch
Art Direction and Design: Jessica Rogers
Production: Jeannette Bailey, Caryl Boyer, Kristi Lively, Cynthia Stiles
Vignettes on pages 94–97 by Flavia Conley

*To Joshua Weisberg,
with thanks*

Meet the WellieWishers

The WellieWishers are a group of fun-loving girls who each have the same big, bright wish: to be a good friend. They love to play in a large and leafy backyard garden cared for by Willa's Aunt Miranda.

Willa

Ashlyn

Emerson

When the WellieWishers step into their colorful garden boots, also known as wellingtons or *wellies*, they are ready for anything—stomping in mud puddles, putting on a show, and helping friendships grow. Like you, they're learning that being kind, creative, and caring isn't always easy, but it's the best way to make friendships bloom.

Camille

Kendall

Who Is Coming?

The WellieWishers were building something big.

"This is the most fun project we've ever done!" said Ashlyn.

"Yes," agreed Willa. "We'd better hurry up and finish before Mr. Louie brings her."

"When do you think she'll arrive?" asked Camille.

"Sooner than soon," said Emerson.

"I hope."

"Look!" said Kendall, pointing. "Here she comes!"

"Here's your chicken!" said Mr. Louie.
His farm was next to Aunt Miranda's
garden, where the WellieWishers played.
Mr. Louie held up a crate that had a
plucky, clucky, red-and-white hen inside.

"Thank you, Mr. Louie!" said all the
WellieWishers.

"Her name is Queen Ruby," said Mr.
Louie.

"Because she has that red comb on her head that looks like a crown," said Willa, who loved birds of all kinds, including chickens.

"That's right," said Mr. Louie, smiling at Willa.

"Welcome, Queen Ruby," said Ashlyn. She curtsied as if the hen were a real queen. "We've never had a queen in our garden before."

Queen Ruby tilted her head and blinked her bright black eyes as if to say, "Thank you. I'm glad to be here."

"Oh, I *love* Queen Ruby," gushed Emerson. "She's *won*derful!"

Kendall said, "Look, Queen Ruby, we built you a chicken coop."

"I decorated your feeder with flowers, your majesty," said Ashlyn.

"I made you a nest," said Willa. "I hope you like it."

"Did you see the weather vane on top of your coop?" Camille asked Queen Ruby.

"I made this apron," said Emerson. "It has two eggs and a little chick." She twirled to show her apron to Queen Ruby.

Gently, Mr. Louie placed Queen Ruby on top of her nest. Then he said to the girls, "You've thought of everything that Queen Ruby might need, and you've made a real nice home for her. I'm sure as sunshine that she'll be happy here."

Queen Ruby ruffled her feathers, wiggled her bottom, and sat up straight on her nest. She looked as pleased and proud as a queen on a throne.

"Keep a close eye on Queen Ruby, girls," said Mr. Louie. "She might lay eggs. If she does, she has to stay on her nest and keep the eggs warm for three weeks. Only then can the eggs hatch, so that you'll have—"

"Baby chicks!" the WellieWishers shouted.

"That's right," nodded Mr. Louie. "Peeping, cheeping baby chicks." He handed the girls a book about chickens. "If you have any questions, look in this book."

"Thank you, Mr. Louie," said the girls. "We'll take good care of Queen Ruby. We promise."

They waved as he drove away, calling out, "Thank you! We love Queen Ruby! Thank you for bringing her to us!"

The WellieWishers gathered around
the chicken coop to admire Queen Ruby.

Emerson sang a song she made up to the tune of "Twinkle, Twinkle, Little Star." She danced for Queen Ruby as she sang:

> *Good Queen Ruby, feel at home!*
> *Fluff your feathers. Wave your comb.*
> *Eat your feed and stretch your legs.*
> *Soon we hope you'll lay some eggs.*
> *Good Queen Ruby, we love you,*
> *And we'll love your babies, too!*

The next day, when the girls went to take care of Queen Ruby, they found . . .

"An egg!" breathed Camille.

"Ooooh," sighed all the girls in awe.

"Good job, your majesty," said Ashlyn to the hen.

Queen Ruby blinked and lifted her beak in a queenly manner.

"Don't forget to go back to your nest and sit on your egg," Willa said. "Otherwise, it won't hatch."

When the girls came to see Queen Ruby the next day, there was another egg in the nest. And the next day after that, there was another!

"Queen Ruby, you are a superstar," said Kendall. "You deserve your crown."

Queen Ruby ruffled her feathers. *Puck, puck, puck,* she clucked, as if to say, "Well, of course!"

"Remember what Mr. Louie told us," cautioned Willa. "We have to take good care of Queen Ruby so that she can take good care of her eggs. She must keep them warm until they hatch."

"We'll give Queen Ruby royal treatment," said Ashlyn.

Willa made sure that Queen Ruby always had straw for her nest.

Ashlyn made sure that Queen Ruby always had water to drink.

Camille made sure that Queen Ruby always had chicken feed to eat.

Kendall made sure that Queen Ruby always had a nice, clean coop.

Emerson made sure that Queen Ruby always had entertainment. She danced and sang to the tune of "Twinkle, Twinkle, Little Star":

Sit, Queen Ruby, be our guest.
Keep your eggs warm in your nest.
Help them hatch out pretty quick.
Soon you'll have some baby chicks!
Good Queen Ruby, we love you,
And we'll love your babies, too!

Chapter 2

Princess
Peep

Mr. Louie said it takes three weeks for eggs to hatch," said Willa.

"I like your song, Emerson," said Ashlyn. "But when you sing, 'Help them hatch out pretty quick,' your words are wrong. Three weeks doesn't seem 'pretty quick' to me. It feels like a long time."

"Think how long it must feel to poor Queen Ruby," said Camille. "She's the one who has to sit on the eggs!"

"And I bet those eggs are bumpy under her bottom," said Kendall. "It must be like sitting on golf balls."

"That's why I sing and dance for

Queen Ruby," said Emerson, spinning on one toe. "So she won't be bored."

Emerson sang her song again, but she changed the words a little bit:

> *Stay, Queen Ruby, on your nest.*
> *Though it does not feel the best.*
> *When your eggs hatch in three weeks,*
> *We will hear some cheery cheeps.*
> *Good Queen Ruby, we love you,*
> *And we'll love your babies, too!*

At last, after three weeks, the girls and Aunt Miranda heard a new sound coming from the chicken coop: *peep, peep, peep.*

The peeping grew louder when

Queen Ruby moved and uncovered one of her eggs. "Oh," sighed Willa. "The peeping is coming from inside that egg. It's going to hatch!"

"Finally," whispered Ashlyn, as Queen Ruby stood up to fluff her feathers and stretch her legs.

"Come on, baby chick," Kendall said to the peeping egg. "You can do it!"

First, the chick
pecked a little hole
from inside the
eggshell with its beak.
Pickety-pickety-pick!

Then the chick
made the hole bigger.
Peckety-peckety-peck!

Next, the egg cracked.
C-r-r-r-a-a-a-c-k!

After that, the egg wobbled. *Wobbledy-wobbledy-wobble.*

And then at last, the chick pushed itself out and said hello! *Peep-peep-peep! Beep-beep-beep! Cheep-cheep-cheep!*

"The chick is kind of wet and scrawny, isn't it?" said Kendall, staring at the wobbly-headed chick.

"Well, it's just born!" said Emerson. She knelt down so that she was eye-to-eye with the chick. She sang:

Happy birthday to you,
Happy birthday to you.
Happy birthday, baby chicken,
Happy birthday to you!

"Congratulations, Queen Ruby," said Ashlyn. "Now you have a little princess chick."

Queen Ruby gave a royal bow. She strutted around the coop looking very pleased with herself.

Peep, peeped the baby chick. *Peep, peep, peep.*

"You're a very good peeper," Emerson said to the chick. "We'll call you Princess Peep."

Peep, peep, peep, answered Princess Peep.

But the more the little chick peeped, the less she sounded like a princess. Instead, she sounded like a poor, pitiful baby chick calling out to its mother.

"Okay, Queen Ruby!" Willa said. "It's time to get back on your nest now. You are a mother hen." Willa looked in the book that Mr. Louie gave the girls. "The book says that Princess Peep needs to be kept warm until her feathers fluff. And your other two eggs need to be kept warm as well so that they can hatch, too."

But Queen Ruby seemed to think that her work was done. She showed no interest in getting back on her nest, not even when Kendall patted the nest and called, "Here, Ruby, Ruby, Ruby. Come!"

Queen Ruby ignored Kendall and strolled out into the sunshine.

Puny Princess Peep shivered unhappily.

"Oh, you poor little thing," cried Emerson, putting her nose near the baby chick's beak.

Willa looked in the book again. "It says in this book that a chick has to be kept warm—really warm, about one hundred degrees—or it will die," she said.

"Oh, no," wailed all the girls. "We've got to save her. What can we do?"

"We'll have to make an incubator for her in the greenhouse," said Aunt Miranda.

"What's an incubator?" asked Kendall.

"It's a special box that's kept warm by a heat lamp," explained Willa. She held up the book to show the picture of the incubator to the girls.

"But what about the other two eggs?" asked Camille. "Queen Ruby is ignoring them. She is not keeping them warm now that she's hatched one egg."

"The book says that sometimes hens get distracted. Maybe Queen Ruby will get back on her nest if we take Princess Peep away," said Willa. "Emerson, you stay here at the chicken coop with Queen Ruby and Princess Peep. When the incubator is ready, we'll move Princess Peep to the greenhouse. Come on, everybody, we have to hurry."

Chapter 3

A Yellow Puff
of Downy Fluff

Emerson was glad to stay behind with Princess Peep. She made up new words to the tune of "Twinkle, Twinkle, Little Star":

> *Little princess, we love you!*
> *And we know just what to do.*
> *You'll be warm and you'll be fed,*
> *In the greenhouse, in your bed.*
> *Princess Peep, how we love you.*
> *Pretty soon you'll love us, too.*

In a little while, Kendall came back to the chicken coop. "The incubator is ready," she said.

Very carefully, Emerson carried Princess Peep to the greenhouse.

Emerson set Princess Peep into the incubator box very gently.

"Welcome to your new home, Princess Peep," said Ashlyn.

Kendall, Camille, Ashlyn, and Willa had worked hard to prepare the incubator in the greenhouse. Aunt Miranda gave them a lamp to keep the incubator box warm and full of light. The girls lined the bottom of the box with a layer of clean, fresh-smelling pine shavings. They hung a thermometer in the box so that they could be sure the incubator was always nice and cozy.

Princess Peep seemed to be pleased
with her new home. *Peep!* she peeped.
"I told you that you'd
like it," said Emerson.

In the cozy incubator box, Princess Peep's downy feathers dried. She grew fluffy and round. Her eyes were bright.

"Princess Peep," said Camille, "you are a yellow puff of downy fluff!"

The girls loved to watch the little chick. She'd peep and cheep, and peck and drink, and hip and hop. Then she'd take a short nap, wake up, and do everything all over again!

"She's just as cute when she's sleeping as she is when she's peeping," said Ashlyn fondly.

During one of Princess Peep's naps, the girls tiptoed away and went to the chicken coop to care for Queen Ruby.

"Oh, thank goodness, Queen Ruby is back on her nest," said Kendall, relieved.

"I guess now that Princess Peep is out of her sight, Queen Ruby isn't distracted," said Camille. "She's back to business, sitting on her two eggs."

"Good work, your majesty," Ashlyn said.

"Those two eggs should hatch soon," said Willa. "Either today or tomorrow."

Chirpety-chirpety-chirp! Queen Ruby chirped, as if she were telling her eggs, "Hurry up and hatch!"

Chapter 4

Hello,
Yellow Shadow

But the next morning when the WellieWishers checked the chicken coop, Queen Ruby's eggs still had not hatched. So the girls went to the greenhouse to take care of Princess Peep.

Camille made sure that Princess Peep had mash to eat. Kendall made sure that Princess Peep had clean pine shavings in her box. Ashlyn made sure that Princess Peep had water to drink.

And Emerson put on a puppet show for Princess Peep. She told chicken jokes and riddles.

Which side of Princess Peep has the most feathers? The outside!

Why does Princess Peep hide? Because she is a little chicken.

How does Queen Ruby tell time? One o'cluck, two o'cluck . . .

Peep, peep, peep, peeped Princess Peep. "She's peeping at your jokes, Emerson," smiled Ashlyn. "I think she likes them."

"Of course!" said Emerson. "She thinks my jokes are *egg*-cellent!"

The next day, when the girls went to the chicken coop to say good morning to Queen Ruby, they saw that the eggs *still* hadn't hatched.

"Queen Ruby must be getting discouraged," said Emerson. While the other girls went to the greenhouse to take care of Princess Peep, Emerson sang to encourage Queen Ruby:

> *Stay, Queen Ruby, on your nest.*
> *Though it does not feel the best.*
> *Hatch your eggs out soon today,*
> *And we all will shout, "Hooray!"*
> *Good Queen Ruby, we love you!*
> *And we'll love your babies, too.*

Pawk, pawk, agreed Queen Ruby.

In the greenhouse, Willa said, "Oh, dear! Princess Peep looks unhappy this morning."

"I think she looks sick," said Kendall.

"I'll go get the vet set and examine poor Princess Peep," said Camille.

Ashlyn sighed, "I sure hope Princess Peep is okay."

Camille was back in a flash with the vet set.

Very gently and carefully, Camille listened to Princess Peep's heart, looked at Princess Peep's eyes, and touched Princess Peep's feet.

Princess Peep drooped. She moped moodily on the pine shavings, looking depressed. She didn't make even the tiniest peep.

Just then, Emerson skipped into the greenhouse. She was singing:

Little princess, here I am,
With some puppets on my hands!

"Shh!" Ashlyn interrupted her in a whisper. "Princess Peep doesn't feel good today."

"What's the matter?" asked Emerson. She peered over the top of the incubator. "What's up, Princess?" she asked.

Leaning over the box, Emerson waggled the puppets on her hands. "Hello, Princess Peep," said Emerson.

The moment Princess Peep saw Emerson, the chick lifted her head, blinked her dark eyes, and began to cheep for joy. *Peep, peep, peep, peep, peep, peep, peep!*

Then Princess Peep hopped into her mash and splattered her water, cheeping merrily, *Peep peep, cheep cheep, beep beep!*

"She looks fine to me," said Emerson.

The other girls stared at Emerson in awe.

"Wow," Ashlyn said. "You cured Princess Peep, Emerson. How did you do that?"

Emerson shrugged. "I guess she likes me," she said.

Willa said, "She sure does! In fact, I think she has imprinted on you."

"What does imprinted mean?" Camille asked.

"It means that after a chick hatches, it thinks that the first big shape it sees is its mother," said Willa. "Princess Peep saw Emerson first, so she imprinted on her."

Kendall nodded and said, "Emerson, she loves you."

"Well, I love her right back," said Emerson. "She's a wonderful chicken." Then Emerson said, "Princess Peep's water bowl is dirty, and her mash is all scattered, and she needs fresh pine shavings. I'll play with her while you guys clean up."

"Here, I'll take her out of her box," said Ashlyn.

"No," said Emerson. She lifted the squiggly, wiggly chick and cuddled her next to her cheek. "Princess Peep wants to be with me."

Emerson set the little chick down on the floor of the greenhouse. When Emerson took a step to get out of Kendall's way, *hop!* Princess Peep took a step, too. Emerson took another step, and another. Princess Peep followed her. *Hop, hop!*

"Watch this!" Emerson crowed to the other girls. She and Princess Peep paraded—*step, hop, step, hop, step, hop*—across the greenhouse floor. Princess Peep followed Emerson like a little yellow shadow.

"Isn't it cute how Princess Peep follows Emerson?" said Camille.

"Yes," said Kendall as she scrubbed the little chick's bowl. "I wish Princess Peep had imprinted on me."

"Me, too," said Ashlyn, who was refilling Princess Peep's mash bowl.

"Emerson is lucky," sighed Willa.

"Queen Ruby wasn't a careful mother," said Camille. "She didn't keep Princess Peep warm. So it's good that Princess Peep imprinted on Emerson instead."

"I guess so," said Willa. "Still, Emerson is usually more interested in singing and dancing and putting on puppet shows. It's weird to think of Emerson as—"

"A mother hen!" Camille and Willa said together, giggling.

When the girls finished cleaning Princess Peep's incubator box, Emerson put the chick back in it. She sang a lullaby to the tune of "Twinkle, Twinkle, Little Star":

> *Little princess, go to sleep.*
> *Do not make a single peep.*
> *When you wake up, we'll have fun.*
> *We're each other's favorite one.*
> *But right now you have to sleep.*
> *Please don't make a single peep.*

The little chick nestled into the pine shavings, all tired out from following Emerson around the greenhouse.

Ashlyn began to say, "Let's—"

"Shh!" Emerson shushed her. "Princess Peep is going to sleep."

"Sorry," whispered Ashlyn. She continued softly, "Let's go play hopscotch in the garden."

"Okay," said the rest of the girls.

Emerson leaned over the incubator box and gave Princess Peep an air kiss. "Bye-bye, sweetie pie," she said softly.

But the moment Princess Peep spied Emerson, the little chick began to fuss.

Pee-yee-yeep! Princess Peep cried. *Peep, beep, cheep, peep, peep, cheep, beep!*

"She doesn't want to be alone," said Camille. "I'll stay here and hold her." She leaned forward to lift Princess Peep out of the box.

Pee-yee-yeep-yeep-yeep! Princess Peep cried again, louder than before.

Camille stepped back. "She doesn't want me," said Camille. "She wants you, Emerson."

"Of course she does," said Emerson. She reached into the box and stroked Princess Peep's soft down.

"We'll wait till she falls asleep," said Ashlyn. "Then you can come play hopscotch, too."

"That's all right," said Emerson. "You go ahead. I'll catch up later."

Emerson watched the other girls skip off happily to play hopscotch. She could hear them laughing and talking. Emerson looked down at Princess Peep.

"I'm going to sing your lullaby again," she said to the little chick. "And this time, I want you to go to sleep. Do you hear me?"

Peep, said Princess Peep.

Emerson sang to the chick, and then looked to see if Princess Peep was asleep. But Princess Peep was wide awake. She cheeped and beeped and hopped in her box.

"All right," said Emerson, lifting the little chick and putting her on the floor. "We can go for a walk around the greenhouse. I hope that will tire you out."

At first, Princess Peep followed Emerson. But then, when Emerson wasn't watching her, the frisky little chick hopped under a shelf, got lost behind a stack of flowerpots, and couldn't find her way out!

Pee-yee-yeep! peeped poor, frightened Princess Peep.

"Where are you?" cried Emerson, alarmed.

Peep! called Princess Peep.

Emerson got down on her hands and knees. She saw Princess Peep's fluffy yellow head peeking around an overturned flowerpot. "Don't worry. I've got you," said Emerson. She stretched her arm to reach for the chick, but just then . . .

Wind dashed into the greenhouse yelling, "Emerson, come quick! The eggs are hatching!"

Bam! Emerson sat up so quickly that she banged her head on the shelf. *Crash!* Over went the shelf. *Smash!* Down fell the flowerpots. Petals and leaves and dirt and stems and flowers went flying. *Clank!* The watering can tumbled, splashing water all over everything, but mostly on Emerson.

"I can't come," Emerson wailed to Willa. "I've got to rescue Princess Peep. She's stuck under here. And now I've made a mess!"

Willa was already running off to the chicken coop. "Hurry up," she called back to Emerson. "Or you'll miss it all!"

Chapter 5

Birds of a Feather

Where's Emerson?" Camille asked when Willa ran up to the chicken coop.

"She can't leave Princess Peep," said Willa.

"Aw, that's too bad," said Kendall. "She should be here to sing 'Happy Birthday' to the new chicks."

"Oh, look!" said Ashlyn.

The girls watched, breathless, as

pickety-pickety-pick, the chicks pecked
holes from inside their eggshells.
Then *peckety-peckety-peck*, they made
the holes bigger. Then *c-r-r-a-a-a-ck*,
the eggs cracked. Then *wobbledy-
wobbledy-wobble*, the eggs wobbled.
Then, at last . . .

Peep-peep-peep! Beep-beep-beep! Cheep-cheep-cheep! The chicks pushed themselves out and said hello.

"Congratulations, Queen Ruby," said Ashlyn. "You have two new chicks."

Pawk! said Queen Ruby proudly. She fluffed her feathers and hunkered down on her nest.

"Good! This time, Queen Ruby is staying on her nest and keeping her hatchlings warm," said Kendall. "Let's go tell Emerson the good news."

"Princess Peep has two sisters," Ashlyn announced. "And Queen Ruby is right on top of them, keeping them cozy!"

"Oh, I'm glad," said Emerson. She sounded tired.

"We're sorry you missed the eggs hatching," said Camille.

"Me, too," sighed Emerson.

"What's the matter, Emerson?" asked Willa kindly.

Emerson looked over at Princess Peep, who was finally asleep in her box. "Being a mother hen is hard," Emerson said. "I love Princess Peep, but taking care of her is a big responsibility. I felt terrible when she got stuck behind the flowerpots! What if she had been hurt? It would have been my fault."

"She's fine," said Kendall, patting Emerson's arm.

Emerson shook her head. "At first, I was so happy that Princess Peep imprinted on me and loved me best,"

she admitted. "But now, well, I'm tired of being a mother hen."

"I think we can help you," said Willa. She was looking at the book from Mr. Louie. "This book tells how to return a chick to its mother after they have been separated. Do you want to try it?"

"As long as Princess Peep will be safe and happy," said Emerson.

"Okay," said Willa. "We'll meet at the chicken coop—" She checked the book again, and then said, "Tonight."

That night, Aunt Miranda and the girls brought Princess Peep to the chicken coop. Queen Ruby and the two newly hatched chicks were sleeping. Carefully, Aunt Miranda slipped Princess Peep into the nest under Queen Ruby.

Pawk? clucked Queen Ruby, half opening her eyes.

The girls and Aunt Miranda held their breath. Queen Ruby rustled her feathers a bit, and then closed her eyes and went back to sleep.

"Phew," sighed Kendall.

"Do you think she'll notice there are three chicks in her nest now?" asked Camille.

"We won't know until the morning," said Willa. "We'll just have to wait and see."

The next morning, the girls
hurried to the chicken coop.

"The plan worked!" said
Kendall. "Queen Ruby is being
a mother to Princess Peep, just
as we hoped."

Queen Ruby tilted her head and stared at the girls with her bright black eyes. *Pawk!* she said in her most queenly manner. Her three little chicks peeked their heads out from beneath her. They all chirped hello happily. Then Queen Ruby gently nudged them back under her feathers.

"Princess Peep likes being here with Queen Ruby and the other chicks," said Willa. "It's like the old saying, 'Birds of a feather flock together.'"

"Are you sad that Princess Peep likes Queen Ruby and the chicks more than she likes you?" Camille asked Emerson.

"No," said Emerson. She grinned. "I'll always love Princess Peep. She's fun, but you guys are more fun and a lot less work and worry!" Emerson sang:

> You can be a chicken's friend,
> But don't be its mother hen!
> Chicks are cute and lots of fun,
> Peeping, cheeping, on the run.
> But for friends both smart and sweet,
> WellieWishers can't be beat!

Caretaking

Like Emerson, your child can learn about nurturing by helping to care for plants and animals. Care-taking gives a child a sense of responsibility and helps form strong relationships. And it's fun! Encourage your girl to flex her nurturing muscles with these activities:

Seed, Sprout, Blossom!

Grow a plant from seed to sprout. Begin by helping your daughter paint a six-inch pot with tempera or acrylic paints. (Be sure the pot has a hole in the bottom and a dish underneath to catch water.) Help her fill the pot with

soil and plant a few seeds. Peas and beans sprout quickly, have visible flowers, and produce edible veggies. Nasturtium flowers have large, easy-to-handle seeds and grow fast. Plus, their bright, colorful blooms are edible in salads! Find a sunny spot in your house where your daughter can water her sprout and watch it grow.

Animal Helper

Call or visit a local animal shelter or humane society and ask what the shelter needs. Most animal shelters gladly accept donations of towels, small blankets, pet food, animal litter, and dog or cat toys. Make a list with your girl, and gather items to donate. You can find the items at a store, but you also might have things around the house that you could donate, such as old towels, tennis balls, or baby blankets. Knowing that she is helping animals in need will make your girl feel very good.

Creative Egg-tivities

Let Emerson's story inspire your "chick" with these easy egg-themed crafts:

Musical Maracas

For these rhythm-makers, you'll need:

- 2 plastic eggs (the kind that open)
- Popcorn kernels or rice, uncooked
- 4 plastic spoons
- Masking tape or washi tape
- Stickers (optional)

Fill one half of a plastic egg with popcorn kernels or rice, and close the egg tightly. With one pair of spoons facing each other, tape the handles of the spoons together at the bottom. Place the plastic egg between the bowls of the two spoons, and wrap with tape to secure the egg in place. Decorate with stickers if desired. Repeat with the second egg and pair of spoons. Then turn on some music and shake the maracas to the beat!

Egg Carton Caterpillar

For this classic craft, you'll need:

- Egg carton
- Scissors
- Tempera paints in assorted colors
- Dark marker or 2 adhesive dots and 2 googly eyes
- Thin straws or chenille stems

Help your daughter cut off a single row of six "humps" from the egg carton, keeping the humps connected in one piece. Paint each hump with a different color, and let dry. Make two eyes at the end of the row with the marker, or attach googly eyes with adhesive dots. Use a pencil to poke two small holes above the eyes. Cut two straws or pieces of chenille stem, and insert them into the holes to make antennae.

About the Author

VALERIE TRIPP says that she became
a writer because of the kind of person she is.
She says she's curious, and writing requires you
to be interested in everything. Talking is her
favorite sport, and writing is a way of talking
on paper. She's a daydreamer, which helps her
come up with her ideas. And she loves words.
She even loves the struggle to come up
with just the right words as she writes
and rewrites. Ms. Tripp lives in
Maryland with her husband.

Here are some more WellieWisher books to read!

The Riddle of the Robin

A robin has moved into the garden, thrilling the WellieWishers with its pretty songs. When the girls bring it presents, they learn what robins like to eat. (Hint: It's sort of like spaghetti!) Then one day, the robin disappears. The girls go on a hunt to find it—and get a major surprise! Can animal-lover Willa figure out what's up with her new feathered friend?

Ashlyn's Unsurprise Party

Ashlyn is throwing a party! She wants to keep everything top secret so that she can surprise her friends. Then she learns that her friends have allergies and other needs. At first, Ashlyn is disappointed about letting her friends in on her secret plans— but it turns out that Ashlyn is in for the biggest surprise of all!

The Muddily-Puddily Show

The WellieWishers are putting on a show, and Emerson is in charge. The girls love her songs and silly skits, but not all of Emerson's creative ideas are working. Ashlyn can't see out of her pumpkin costume, Willa has a touch of stage fright, and Kendall is struggling with the special effects. When the girls try to tell her their problems, Emerson doesn't listen. Will the show go on?

Camille's Mermaid Tale

Camille loves the ocean—the warm sand, the pretty shells, and the sparkling waves that tickle her toes. Sometimes she even imagines that she's a mermaid with whales and dolphins for friends! When the other WellieWishers see how much Camille misses her summers by the sea, they want to help . . . but how can four girls turn a garden into an ocean?

The Rainstorm Brainstorm

It's Aunt Miranda's birthday! The WellieWishers want to give her something special, but they can't agree on what it should be. Then Kendall discovers the Tomorrow Pile. What looks like a bunch of old, dirty, broken things to the other girls looks like cool stuff with lots of potential to Kendall! Can the girls use it to make something wonderful?

The Mystery of Mr. E

There's a new friend in the garden—a big, shaggy dog with the mysterious name of Mr. E! The dog loves to play, so when it suddenly disappears, the WellieWishers are worried. They search high and low and find paw prints, but no dog. What has happened to Mr. E? The WellieWishers are about to get the surprise of their life!